THE EMPTY CREEL

THE EMPTY CREEL

BY
GERALDINE POPE

ILLUSTRATED BY
DENNIS CUNNINGHAM

DAVID R. GODINE, PUBLISHER
BOSTON

FIRST PUBLISHED IN 1995 BY
DAVID R. GODINE, PUBLISHER, INC.
P.O. BOX 9103
LINCOLN, MA 01773

LIBRARY OF CONGRESS CATALOGING -IN - PUBLICATION DATA
POPE, GERALDINE 1961-
THE EMPTY CREEL / BY GERALDINE POPE ; ILLUSTRATED BY DENNIS CUNNINGHAM
P.   CM.

SUMMARY: LUCY AND HER GRANDFATHER FISH TOGETHER OFTEN AND SHE
DREAMS OF SOMEDAY CATCHING A REALLY BIG FISH, BUT GRANDPA TEACHES
HER THAT FISHING IS ABOUT MORE THAN THE DAY'S CATCH.

ISBN 1-56792-044-6

[1. FISHING -- FICTION. 2. GRANDFATHERS -- FICTION.] I. CUNNINGHAM,
DENNIS, ILL. II. TITLE.
PZ7.P7925E M 1995
[E] -- DC20   95 - 15703
CIP
AC

THE EMPTY CREEL

SOME SATURDAYS, GRANDPA COMES OVER EARLY IN THE MORNING AND SAYS TO ME, "GRAB YOUR GREEN BOOTS, LUCY. WE'RE GOING FISHING!"

I SQUEAL, "YIPPEE!" AS LOUD AS I CAN AND RUN UPSTAIRS TO GET MY BOOTS AND THE BROWN WICKER CREEL HE GAVE ME. "WE'LL BE BACK FOR DINNER!" GRANDPA PROMISES MY MOTHER AS WE HEAD OUT THE DOOR.

WHEN WE GET TO THE RIVER, GRANDPA CARRIES THE TACKLE BOX AND OUR TWO FISHING RODS OVER TO THE BOAT. I LUG MY CREEL AND THE THINGS THAT MAMA MAKES ME BRING, LIKE AN EXTRA SWEATER, MY LUNCH, AND SUN BLOCK.

THEN I HEAD OVER
TO SEE MYRON, WHO WORKS AT
THE GAS DOCK.

GRANDPA MOTORS OVER TO GET GAS, THEN HELPS ME INTO THE BOAT. AS WE PUSH AWAY FROM THE DOCK, MYRON SAYS, "DON'T GET SKUNKED TODAY, LUCY!" GRANDPA HEADS FOR OUR FAVORITE SPOT AT MOSS ROCK. HE DODGES THE WHIRLPOOLS. I WATCH FOR ROCKS. THE OUTBOARD GROANS AS IT WORKS AGAINST THE CURRENT.

GRANDPA SLOWS DOWN AS WE GET
CLOSE TO MOSS ROCK,
A BIG BOULDER THAT'S COVERED
WITH BRIGHT GREEN MOSS.

HE ZIGS AND ZAGS THE BOAT AND
FINALLY SETTLES US THERE.
THE MOUNTAINS POINT
STEEPLE- STRAIGHT TO THE SKY.
BURNT PATCHES OF DOUGLAS FIR
REMIND ME OF HIS
WHISKERS.

GRANDPA HANDS ME MY ROD.
I STAND UP AND CAREFULLY TAKE THE
HOOK OUT OF THE CORK HANDLE.
TRYING TO REMEMBER EVERYTHING
GRANDPA HAS TAUGHT ME,
I PULL THE LINE OFF
MY REEL EIGHT TIMES.
I'M CAREFUL NOT TO TANGLE THE LINE.
"THAT'S MY GIRL,"
SAYS GRANDPA PROUDLY.

WE DON'T SAY ANYTHING FOR AWHILE. WE WAIT. AS I WATCH MY LURE TWIRL BRIGHTLY THROUGH SWIRLING, GREEN WATER, I JUST KNOW THAT A BIG SALMON IS LURKING IN THE SHADE OF OUR BOAT, WATCHING.

BUT HE DOESN'T.

GRANDPA SAYS THAT WHEN HE WAS
A BOY, THE RIVER WAS
SO THICK WITH SALMON,
THAT YOU COULD WALK
ACROSS THE WATER ON THEIR BACKS.

STARING AT MY LINE,
I DREAM OF A FISH SO BIG
THAT IT PULLS OUR BOAT BEHIND IT.

"HOLD ON, LUCY!" CRIES GRANDPA.

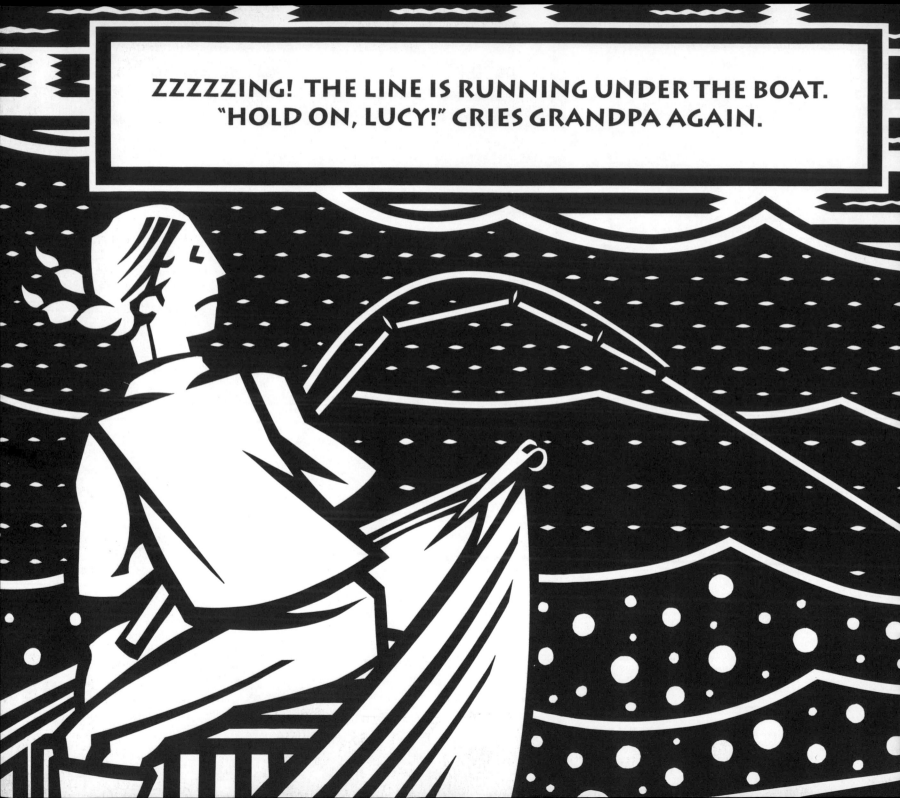

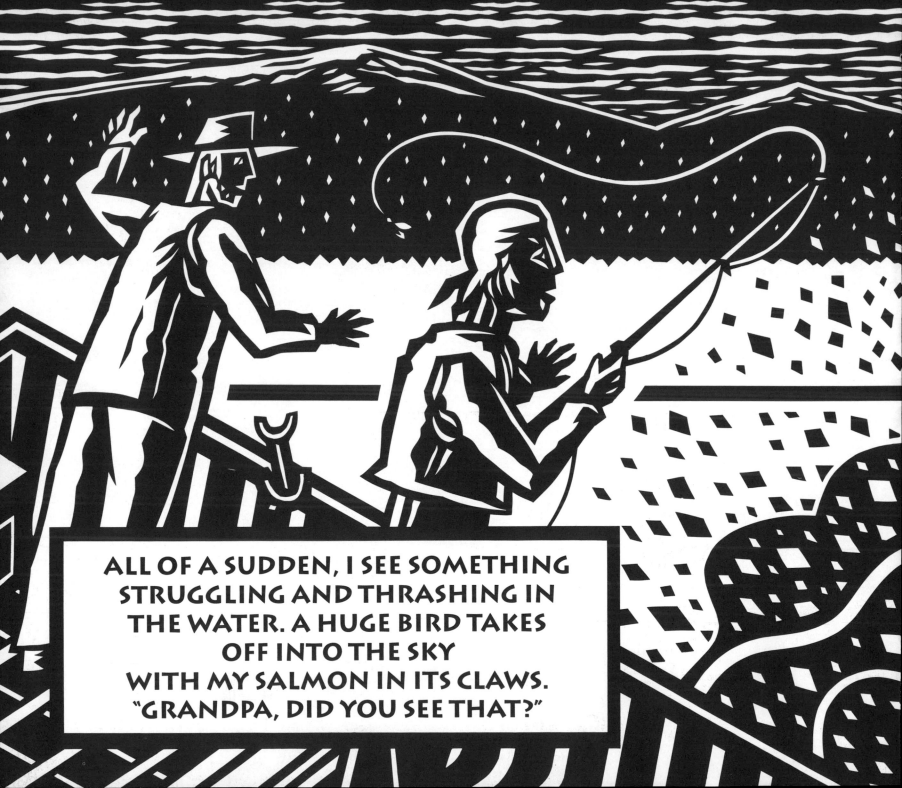

"MAGNIFICENT!" CRIES GRANDPA.
"AN OSPREY,
THE BEST FISHERMAN OF ALL!"

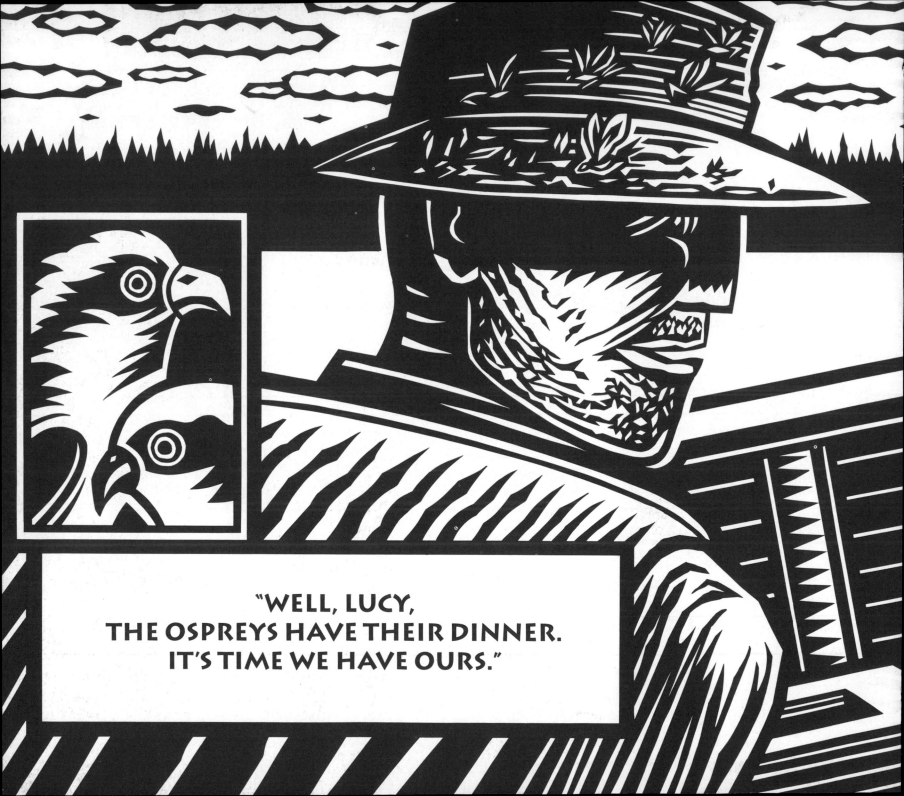

GRANDPA SAYS, "IT'S GETTING LATE." HE PUTS THE OUTBOARD INTO GEAR AND TELLS HIS SAME STORIES ABOUT GRIZZLY BEARS, ORCA WHALES AND SEALS FISHING FOR SALMON.

ON THE WAY BACK TO THE TRUCK,
I ASK GRANDPA, "AREN'T YOU SAD THAT
WE DIDN'T CATCH THAT BIG FISH?"
HE SQUEEZES BOTH OF MY SHOULDERS.
"LUCY, MY GIRL," HE SAYS,
"WE MAY RETURN WITH AN EMPTY CREEL,
BUT WE COME HOME WITH FULL HEARTS."

GERALDINE POPE
HAS WRITTEN FOR NEWSPAPERS
AND MAGAZINES IN THE
UNITED STATES
AND EUROPE.
SHE CURRENTLY LIVES IN
CAMAS, WASHINGTON,
WITH HER THREE CHICKENS,
FOUR CHILDREN,
FIVE HORSES,
AND
TWELVE HOUNDS.

DENNIS CUNNINGHAM,
WHO IS BOTH
A FISHERMAN AND AN ARTIST,
HAS EXHIBITED EXTENSIVELY
THROUGHOUT THE
WESTERN UNITED STATES
AND ABROAD.
"THE EMPTY CREEL"
IS HIS FIRST ILLUSTRATED BOOK.
HE LIVES IN
PORTLAND, OREGON

THE EMPTY CREEL
WAS SET IN
ADOBE LITHOS,
A MEMBER OF ADOBE'S
MODERN ANCIENTS FONTS.
NAMED FOR THE GREEK WORD FOR STONE,
LITHOS CAPTURES THE SPIRIT OF
INSCRIPTIONS CARVED AS EARLY AS
400 B.C. BY THE ANCIENT GREEKS.
THIS CONTEMPORARY
INTERPRETATION WAS
CREATED BY THE BEAUTIFUL & TALENTED
CAROL TWOMBLY.
THE PAPER IS A
COUGAR ACID-FREE SHEET
AND THE BOOK WAS PRINTED BY
DAAMEN,INC.
OF
WEST RUTLAND,
VERMONT.

THE EMPTY CREEL

E   Pope, Geraldine.

           The empty creel.

$17.95

DATE			